This book belongs to

_____

This Book of Mine

Sarah Stewart

Pictures by David Small

FARRAR STRAUS GIROUX / *New York*

To our only granddaughter, Lily

Farrar Straus Giroux Books for Young Readers
An imprint of Macmillan Publishing Group, LLC
120 Broadway, New York, NY 10271

Text copyright © 2019 by Sarah Stewart
Pictures copyright © 2019 by David Small
All rights reserved
Color separations by Bright Arts (H.K.) Ltd.
Printed in China by RR Donnelley Asia Printing Solutions Ltd., Dongguan City, Guangdong
Province
First edition, 2019
1   3   5   7   9   10   8   6   4   2

mackids.com

Library of Congress Cataloging-in-Publication Data

Names: Stewart, Sarah, 1939- author. | Small, David, 1945- illustrator.
Title: This book of mine / Sarah Stewart ; pictures by David Small.
Description: First edition. | New York : Farrar Straus Giroux, 2019. | Summary: Illustrations
    and easy-to-read text celebrate the connection between diverse readers of all ages and the
    books they enjoy.
Identifiers: LCCN 2018039442 | ISBN 9780374305468 (hardcover)
Subjects: CYAC: Books—Fiction.
Classification: LCC PZ7.S84985 Thi 2019 | DDC [E]—dc23
LC record available at https://lccn.loc.gov/2018039442

Our books may be purchased in bulk for promotional, educational, or business use. Please
contact your local bookseller or the Macmillan Corporate and Premium Sales Department
at (800) 221-7945 ext. 5442 or by email at MacmillanSpecialMarkets@macmillan.com.

I take this book . . .

to be my friend.

To chew on it
while you read it.

To grab for it
when I need it.

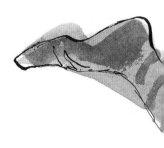

To think about what I
just saw—
then close the book
and try to draw.

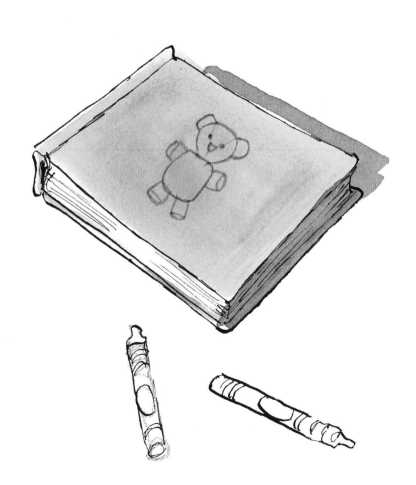

To open it wide
and put my nose inside.

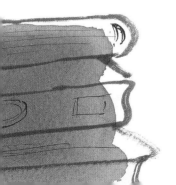

To read it aloud
and wish for a crowd.

To become the book,
now that this book
is mine.

To find knowledge
and happiness . . .

and pleasure.

A treasure for a lifetime,

this book friend of mine.